the
Model Mormon
Mother's Notebook

the
Model Mormon Mother's Notebook

Carol Lynn Pearson
illustrations by John Pearson

CFI
Springville, Utah

ISBN: 1-55517-858-8
e.1

Published by Cedar Fort, Inc.
www.cedarfort.com

Distributed by:

Cover designed by Nicole Williams
Cover design © 2005 by Lyle Mortimer

Printed in the United States of America
10 9 8 7 6 5 4 3 2 1

Printed on acid-free paper

owe to my mother all that was bright and good in my long night.

Helen Keller

Try Judy's idea for getting children ready for church on time—put them to bed Saturday night in their Sunday clothes.

Relief Society assignment:
"Greet husband at door in clean dress."
Buy clean dress!

Return home teachers' phone call—no, the 31st isn't a good night.
Ken has to go home teaching.

The Girl I Used to Be

Back behind the mother in me,
Back behind the wife in me,
There's the girl I used to be,
The girl I think you hardly see
anymore.

She still likes the smell of rain,
Can't resist a country lane,
Listens for the passing train
Covers up a private pain,
like before.

But nobody sees her.
Days go by and nobody speaks her name.
When nobody sees her
She goes inside and closes the door,
Closes the door,
No one can blame her.

So—

See me dust the bookcase there,
Sort the socks to make a pair,
Brush and braid the children's hair,
Take my place at evening prayer,
and then—

Look behind the mother in me,
Look behind the wife in me,
Find the girl I used to be,
The woman she became—
Who needs for you to see
her again.

Carol Lynn Pearson
From "The Dance" musical

If I had the choice of educating a boy or a girl, I would educate the girl. If you educate a boy, you educate one, but if you educate a girl, you educate a generation.

Brigham Young

√ *Weight Watchers*

√ *The Zone*

√ *Slim-Fast*

√ *Dr. Phil*

<u>Try</u> *Winter Quarters diet—roots and berries!*

I mean to lead a simple life, to choose a simple shell I can carry easily—like a hermit crab. But I do not. I find that my frame of life does not foster simplicity. The life I have chosen as wife and mother entrains a whole caravan of complications. . . . My mind reels with it. . . . I must find a balance somewhere between island solitude and communion, between retreat and return.

Anne Morrow Lindbergh
Gift from the Sea

If some of these wonderful women are feeling burdened and grieved by their motherhood instead of rejoicing in it, perhaps it is because they have picked up burdens that are not necessary for them to carry. . . . Guilt is a burden we need not pick up. . . . We must—

- Accept struggle and imperfection as facts of life, not as judgments or punishment.
- Accept many partners in parenting.
- Respect the agency of our children.

Chieko Okazaki

First Aid Panel Wednesday—
Discuss "What puts people into shock?"

—*severe injury*

—*bleeding*

—*excessive loss of fluid*

—motherhood

Don't Push

The minute the doctor said "push"
I did, and I've got to stop now
Because you're eighteen.

Breathe deeply
Think of something else
Don't push
Don't push.

Carol Lynn Pearson

Call Sister C. on topic she assigned me:
"A mother of many children needs to be committed."
How did she mean that?

8

For visiting teaching—
Find out why Sister G. is still depressed

     * Visit her 12 children to see if they know
     * Call her husband in Alaska
        for his opinion

Let your first business be to perform your duties at home. But inasmuch as you are wise stewards . . . you will find that your capacity will increase, and you will be astonished at what you can accomplish.

Eliza R. Snow

The
noblest calling
in the world is motherhood.

True motherhood is the most beautiful of all arts, the greatest of all professions. She who can paint a masterpiece, or who can write a book that will influence millions, deserves the admiration and plaudits of mankind; but she who rears successfully a family of healthy, beautiful sons and daughters, whose immortal souls will exert an influence throughout the ages long after paintings shall have faded, and books and statues shall have decayed or have been destroyed, deserves the highest honor that man can give, and the choicest blessings of God.

David O. McKay

Enrichment challenge—"Try something creative with the children's lunches."
Put peanut butter on <u>after the</u> jelly?

Work on Bishop's challenge to read scriptures for 15 minutes when house is quiet.

Set alarm for 3:30 a.m.

"She that hath clean hands"
—hath not children.

My favorite child—

The one who is ill until she gets well.
The one who is away until he gets home.
The one who is sad until she smiles again.

Anonymous

Suggest mini-class on finance—
"How to Get Back to Where You Were
Five Years Ago"

Other use of wheat—
<u>Throw</u> at weddings

Mother to Child

Look—
Your little fist fits mine
Like the pit in a plum.

One day and one size
These two hands
Will clasp companionably.

Help me, child.
Forgive me when I fail you.
I'm your mother, true,
But in the end
Merely an older equal
Doing her faltering best
For a dear, small friend.

Carol Lynn Pearson

A mother is not a person to lean on, but a
person to make leaning unnecessary.

Dorothy Canfield Fisher

Tell Bishop I need more relief and less society.

Tell Ken that next Sunday I would like to honk the horn while he gets the children ready for church!

Stop waiting to be happy—
    until your car or home is paid off
    until you get a new car or home
    until your new job comes along
    until your kids leave the house
    until you go back to school
    until you finish school
    until you lose 10 lbs.
    until you gain 10 lbs.
    until you get married
    until you get divorced
    until you have kids
    until you retire
    until summer
    until spring
    until winter
    until fall
    until you die

Anonymous

IT IS IN THE HOME that we learn the values by which we guide our lives. That home may be ever so simple. It may be in a poor neighborhood, but with a good father and a good mother, it can become a place of *wondrous upbringing.*

Gordon B. Hinckley

For my contribution to mini-class on getting over depression:

> ~~Have hair done, manicure,~~ pedicure
> ~~Have more children~~
> ~~Take another church job~~
> ~~Bake more often~~
> ✳ *Buy condominium on Waikiki Beach*

Day-Old Child

My day-old child lay in my arms.
With my lips against his ear
I whispered strongly, "How I wish—
I wish that you could hear.

I've a hundred wonderful things to say
(A tiny cough and a nod)
Hurry, hurry, hurry, and grow
So I can tell you about God."

My day-old baby's mouth was still
And my words only tickled his ear.
But a kind of a light passed through his eyes
And I saw this thought appear:

"How I wish I had a voice and words;
I've a hundred things to say.
Before I forget I'd tell you of God—
I left Him yesterday."

Carol Lynn Pearson

The greatest trust that can come to a man and woman is the placing in their keeping the life of a little child.

David O. McKay

The Vow

How could I hide you from hate?
I would, though my arms break with the trying.

Life leans in at the window there
With its bag of dark treasures
Trying for your eyes
So utterly open, so unaware.

You will see men smile over blood
And you will know there is hate.
You may see bombs and butcheries
And you will know there is horror.

Against all this what can I do?
Only vow that before you leave my arms
You will know past ever doubting
That there is love, too.

Carol Lynn Pearson

Housecleaning priority for this week
—Find kitchen counter.

Relief Society challenge—"Commit what time you
can afford to civic involvement."
I will definitely vote in next election.

Life History assignment: "Write down most recent
exciting experience."
* Have exciting experience.

How to preserve children's teeth this Halloween—
1—Send them trick-or-treating from 6-7.
2—From 7-9 give out what they collected.

If, in addition to your wifely and motherly duties, you can pursue one or more fields of public labor . . . all the good that you can accomplish . . . will be so much added glory to your eternal crown.

Brigham Young

IF I HAD MY LIFE TO LIVE OVER . . . I would have gone to bed when I was sick instead of pretending the earth would go into a holding pattern if I weren't there for the day. . . . I would have burned the pink candle sculpted like a rose before it melted in storage. . . . I would have talked less and listened more.

Erma Bombeck

otherhood is more than bearing children. . . . It is the essence of who we are as women.

Sheri Dew

Response for the next time someone asks,
*"Are **all** these children yours?"*
*"**No.** I just checked them out of the library."*

Devise diet you can stick to:
   —*no caviar*
   —*no champagne*
   —*no pina colada cheesecake*
   —*no rutabagas*
Try the Word of Wisdom!

Could a spoonful of—
NutraSweet
Equal
Splenda
   —*help the medicine go down?*
   ✳ *Ask Sister Poppins*

Ask husband if he thinks
I'm becoming less codependent.

Motherhood is near to

divinity

It is the highest, holiest service to be assumed by mankind. It places her who honors its holy calling and service next to the angels.

Heber J. Grant

About the Author

Carol Lynn Pearson is the author of numerous books and plays, among them *Beginnings, The Lesson, Consider the Butterfly, My Turn on Earth, Mother Wove the Morning,* and *Goodbye, I Love You.* As a mother she has committed nearly all of the absurdities found in these pages and is still working toward the ideal. Visit her at www.carollynnpearson.com

About the Illustrator

John Pearson has survived the questionable *Model Mormon Mothering* skills of the writer of this notebook, and has gone on to become a successful animation artist, having worked for *The Simpsons* and Disney. Visit him at www.familiarimage. com